Disney · PIXAR
THE WORLD OF
Cars

D0354359

Look Out for Mater!

Adapted by Andrea Posner-Sanchez
Illustrated by Ivan Boix Estudi

 A GOLDEN BOOK · NEW YORK

Library of Congress Control Number: 2008933270
ISBN: 978-0-7364-2582-7
www.randomhouse.com/kids
Printed in the United States of America
10 9
First Edition

*T*imes had changed in Radiator Springs. Once it was a sleepy little town. Now cars came from all over the world to visit the new racing headquarters of Lightning McQueen. The famous race car liked all the attention he got from his fans. But what he really enjoyed was spending time with his new friends.

Lightning's two closest friends were Mater and Sally.

Mater was a rusty tow truck with a silly sense of humor. He and Lightning McQueen were very different, but they had quickly become best buddies.

Sally was Lightning's "girlyfriend," as
Mater often said. She was caring and smart.
Lightning loved driving around with Sally
by his side.

One day, Sally and Lightning drove to a cliff overlooking a gravel pit. "That seems like a fun place to race," said Lightning. "I'll have to bring Mater there."

"Please don't," Sally begged. "I'm always warning Mater that this place is dangerous. I don't want to worry while I'm out of town the next few days. Promise me you'll look out for Mater while I'm away."

GRAVEL PIT

Back in town, Lightning was sadly rolling along Main Street when Mater came up beside him.

"Aw, shoot! Are you moping 'cause Miss Sally went away?" Mater asked his friend. "You need some Mater-style fu-un!"

Even though Lightning wasn't in the mood, he knew he'd better go along. After all, he had promised Sally he would look out for Mater.

Before long, Mater was speeding toward a grassy hill. "Slow down!" yelled Lightning. But Mater kept on going. The tow truck honked his horn and flew over the hill with a big grin.

Next, Mater drove down a winding dirt road—backward!

"You're crazy!" Lightning called to him. "Turn around!"

"Nah, it's more fun when you're looking the other way," Mater said, chuckling.

As the sun began to set, Mater insisted on going to one last place—the gravel pit!

"We can't go down there," Lightning said. "I promised Sally—"

Before the race car could even finish his sentence, Mater was revving his engine and speeding around the pit.

"Come on down!" cried Mater. "This is fu-un!"

Lightning realized that if he wanted to look out for Mater, he had better stay close to him. So the race car slowly inched his way down the slippery slope.

Mater rushed by, leaving Lightning behind in a cloud of dust.

Just then, the two friends heard a loud "Ahem!" An angry bulldozer was coming up behind them. "Stop messing up my gravel!" he yelled. "This pit is not for playing in!"

Gulp! "Guess it's time to go!" cried Lightning.

"Right behind ya, buddy," replied Mater.

The next day, Mater had a surprise for his friend. Lightning followed Mater to . . . the gravel pit.

"No way!" shouted Lightning. "Let's find a safe place to have fun."

"Shhh," whispered Mater as he rolled past the snoring bulldozer. "Big Bull's sleeping. And anyways, this time we won't even *touch* the gravel."

Before Lightning could stop him, Mater rode onto some rails that had been set up to help move gravel from one end of the pit to the other. The race car watched as Mater zoomed up and down the rails with a big smile on his face. The tow truck honked and hooted as he whooshed around the turns.

Lightning knew he should stop Mater—
he had promised Sally. But it looked like such
fun! Lightning had to try, too.

Lightning made
his way to the top of
the track. He revved
his engine and took off.
"Ka-chow!" It was
fantastic!

"I told ya it was
fu-un!" Mater yelled.

"But Sally's right
about this place being
dangerous," said
Lightning. "Let's get
going before something
goes wrong."

But as the sun began to set, Mater insisted on one more ride. After a while, there was a loud *thwack!*

"You okay, buddy?" Lightning called into the darkness.

Suddenly, a floodlight lit the gravel pit. A booming voice shouted, "What is going on here?" Big Bull had woken up to find Mater hanging by his tow cable!

Luckily, Mater wasn't hurt. But he was stuck. "I can get you down," Big Bull fumed. "But I'll have to break your tow cable to do it."

Once Mater was free, he was as quiet as could be. What kind of tow truck was he without his cable?

Lightning felt bad, too. He should have done a better job looking out for Mater.

The next night, Sally came back to town. "Mater, what happened to you?" she gasped. When she found out that he and Lightning McQueen had been in the gravel pit, she was very angry.

"Lightning tried to warn me," said Mater. "I shoulda been a better friend and listened to him." He started to cry.

"You could have really been hurt," Sally
said. "Thankfully, we can get that tow cable
fixed."

Mater smiled and turned to his red friend.
"Then we can go out for more Mater-style
fu-un!"

Sally frowned. Lightning couldn't help
laughing. "This time, I pick the place.
I'll show you how to have Lightning
McQueen–style fun—*without* getting hurt!"